Animals and Me ABCs

Connie Beyer Horn
Illustrated by Marlene McAuley

CPH®
SAINT LOUIS

To my husband, David.

There are many special things
That the animals do,
From the camels in the desert
To the monkeys in the zoo.

But there is something special
That they can never be.
We'll find out what as we study them
From A to Z.

Alligator, alligator, I know about you.
There's something special only you can do.
You hide in mom's mouth and take a ride,
After hatching from an egg by the riverside.
But there is one thing you can never be,
And that is be a person—just like me.

Butterfly, butterfly, I know about you.
There's something special only you can do.
You spend your early days wrapped up tight;
Then your wings unfold—beautiful and bright.
But there is one thing you can never be,
And that is be a person—just like me.

Camel, camel, I know about you.
There's something special only you can do.
You cross desert sand, but your hooves never sink.
You can walk eight days without a drink!
But there is one thing you can never be,
And that is be a person—just like me.

Dolphin, dolphin, I know about you.
There's something special only you can do.
You send out a signal, and it comes right back.
It measures the distance to your seafood snack.
But there is one thing you can never be,
And that is be a person—just like me.

Elephant, elephant, I know about you.
There's something special only you can do.
Your trunk can pull up trees to clear the land,
Or it can take a peanut from my outstretched hand.
But there is one thing you can never be,
And that is be a person—just like me.

Firefly, firefly, I know about you.
There's something special only you can do.
Fireflies talk with a light that flashes.
They know each other's names by the dots and dashes.
But there is one thing you can never be,
And that is be a person—just like me.

Gorilla, gorilla, I know about you.
There's something special only you can do.
You care for your young like a family
By building your home in a great tall tree.
But there is one thing you can never be,
And that is be a person—just like me.

Honey bee, honey bee, I know about you.
There's something special only you can do;
Bees gather 'round like you're a movie star
As your dance tells them all where the flowers are.
But there is one thing you can never be,
And that is be a person—just like me.

Impala, impala, I know about you.
There's something special only you can do.
When you see a lion or a leopard nearby,
You can jump in the air—ten feet high!
But there is one thing you can never be,
And that is be a person—just like me.

Jaguar, jaguar, I know about you.
There's something special only you can do.
You swim to catch fish, or just for fun,
Then nap on a rock in the South American sun!
But there is one thing you can never be,
And that is be a person—just like me.

Kangaroo, kangaroo, I know about you.
There's something special only you can do.
In Mom's pouch, you play hide and seek.
Joey's three months old when he takes his first peek.
But there is one thing you can never be,
And that is be a person—just like me.

Ladybug, ladybug, I know about you.
There's something special only you can do.
You cover your wings with a bright orange shell
And protect yourself well with a peculiar smell.
But there is one thing you can never be,
And that is be a person—just like me.

Monkey, monkey, I know about you.
There's something special only you can do.
That's why we say, "Monkey see; monkey do!"
But there is one thing you can never be,
And that is be a person—just like me.

Newt, newt, I know about you.
There's something special only you can do.
You lay all your eggs on a bright spring morn,
Folding each one in a leaf till it's time to be born!
But there is one thing you can never be,
And that is be a person—just like me.

Ostrich, ostrich, I know about you.
There's something special only you can do.
Your speedy exit warns that trouble's about,
At eight feet tall, you're a very good scout!
But there is one thing you can never be,
And that is be a person—just like me.

Penguin, penguin, I know about you.
There's something special only you can do.
Momma penguin lays the egg; Dad's the baby-sitter.
He sits for nine long weeks—now that's no quitter!
But there is one thing you can never be,
And that is be a person—just like me.

Quail, quail, I know about you.
There's something special only you can do.
Loving care for each one within your little flock,
Makes you place a "quail guard" around the clock.
But there is one thing you can never be,
And that is be a person—just like me.

Raccoon, raccoon, I know about you.
There's something special only you can do.
You open any lid that's not fastened tight,
When you're out with your babies to hunt at night.
But there is one thing you can never be,
And that is be a person—just like me.

Sea lion, sea lion, I know about you.
There's something special only you can do.
You balance a ball on the end of your nose
And catch every fish that your trainer throws!
But there is one thing you can never be,
And that is be a person—just like me.

Tiger, tiger, I know about you.
There's something special only you can do.
You tip the scale at four hundred pounds,
And catch your lunch—by leaps and bounds.
But there is one thing you can never be,
And that is be a person—just like me.

Sea **U**rchin, sea urchin, I know about you.
There's something special only you can do.
You walk on tiny stilts wherever you go.
Your colors range from blue to red—a pretty rainbow.
But there is one thing you can never be,
And that is be a person—just like me.

Vulture, vulture, I know about you.
There's something special only you can do.
You help our environment by eating dead things
That you find while soaring high on long, wide wings.
But there is one thing you can never be,
And that is be a person—just like me.

Woodchuck, woodchuck, I know about you.
There's something special only you can do.
You predict fair weather is six weeks away
When you see your shadow on Ground Hog Day.
But there is one thing you can never be,
And that is be a person—just like me.

Fo**X**, fox, I know about you.
There's something special only you can do.
Your eyesight is keen; you hear the slightest sound.
That's why so many times you outwit the hounds!
But there is one thing you can never be,
And that is be a person—just like me.

Yucca moth, yucca moth, I know about you.
There's something special only you can do.
Only you can carry pollen on your tiny feet
To make the yucca bloom in the desert heat.
But there is one thing you can never be,
And that is be a person—just like me.

Zebra, zebra, I know about you.
There's something special only you can do.
Your herd slows down for the younger ones
And circles 'round when danger comes.
But there is one thing you can never be,
And that is be a person—just like me.

Yes, there are special things
The animals can do.
But there's one thing for certain,
And I've learned it
through and through.

Animals are a wonder,
But the wondrous thing I see,
Is that God made only one thing
That is just like me ...
And that's ME!

Dear Parent:

As you explore the unique qualities of animals in God's creation, help your child understand his or her own unique gifts and talents. Challenge your child to make animal sounds and try to move like different animals.

Look at baby pictures with your child. Talk about different milestones in your child's development. Place a picture of Jesus in your child's room. Say "Jesus loves you" every time you pass by the picture with your child. Explain that Jesus loved your child enough to give His life. That makes your child a very special person indeed.